For Meg:
In appreciation of
your exuberance
kindness, and brilliance!

Wolfsong

XOX,
Kathryn

Stories by

Kathryn Silver-Hajo

Kathryn Silver-Hajo

ISBN: 978-1-942004-54-7

Library of Congress Control Number: 2023934085

Cover Design by ELJ Editions, Ltd.
Cover Art: "Running the Distance" by Dimitra Milan
(dimitramilan.com)

ELJ Editions, Ltd.
P.O. Box 815
Washingtonville, NY 10992

www.elj-editions.com

Praise for Wolfsong

In *Wolfsong,* her debut collection of stories, Kathryn Silver-Hajo displays her mastery of very short form storytelling. These stories are brilliant bits of sea glass one feels lucky to discover and treasure. Filled with family and food and music, lovers and friends, heartbreak and survival, these stories provide an evocative look at the hard lessons and the singular tender joys of girlhood and womanhood. You'll want to read and reread this beautiful collection and keep it close at hand. It's that good. –Kathy Fish, author of *Wild Life: Collected Works*

With a unique gift for writing about characters whom we feel we have known, Silver-Hajo writes with compassion, and lays bare many worlds of vulnerability, uncertainty, and joy. In these 34 debut stories about the lives of girls, adolescents, and women, she creates a dazzling distillation of experience that is both haunting and hopeful. This is a very fine example of what the flash fiction form can accomplish. The characters in *Wolfsong* nestle deep into our spirits and refuse to let go. –Meg Pokrass, author of *The Loss Detector* and *Spinning to Mars*

The wise stories in *Wolfsong* brilliantly transport the reader from childhood to old age—and teach one of the collection's heartfelt lessons of not wasting a moment "on the poison of disapproval, let alone a lifetime." *Wolfsong* is an inspiring journey every reader should take. –Pamela Painter, author of *Fabrications: New and Selected Stories*

The very short stories in Kathryn Silver-Hajo's *Wolfsong* focus on small, lovely moments in the lives of characters in which everything is illuminated. These are stories that are very much grounded in place and time, but there's also a pervasive sense of *what if* throughout this collection, a tantalizing glimpse of an alternate future and the parallel universe of the imagination. These stories may be small in compass, but they're huge in humor and heart. –Sarah Freligh, author of *Sad Math*

Beautiful and incisive. Each flash in *Wolfsong* is compelling in its own way. Through crisp imagery and lyrical prose, Kathryn Silver-Hajo directs her cast of characters through emotionally resonant stories. Among the female leads you'll find characters who long to belong, others who undergo insufferable tests and some who narrowly escape tragedy, and each aims to steal the show. This debut collection does not disappoint. –Rachel Laverdiere, Former CNF Editor, *Atticus Review, Barren Magazine* and Creator of *Hone and Polish Your Writing* creative writing program

For the loves of my life, Nasser, Bassil, and Naseem

For my little she-wolf Kaya, who is not a wolf at all but believes she is, and who appears in one guise or another throughout this collection

And in memory of my mother-in-law, Alia Zayyat Hajo (1925-2022), whose intrepid life inspired a number of stories in this volume

Contents

Deep In the Woods

Summer weekends were spent in the old farmhouse. My brother and I sitting in the glow of the fire, our parents reading *The Wonderful Wizard of Oz*, the smoky aromas of dinner lingering, cricket-song punctuated by the *snap* of escaping sparks. We'd found a tin box of toys which we gripped as we listened to the story of the lost little girl. When the fire and comforting smells receded and we were tucked in, I listened to the scratch of mice in the walls, drip of rain seeping through musty beams and wondered if the dark might swallow us up.

Up In Smoke

Whenever the fire engines wailed their warnings, Mom came alive, eyes flashing, and Dad glanced up with that far-away smile before drifting back into his head where he mostly lived. But we'd jump into the car with Mom to chase that campfire-gone-mad smell and throbbing red lights. From afar we watched the little men in yellow rubber coats and fireman hats climbing miniature ladders as in a videogame but with real smoke ballooning, brilliant blasts of amber soaring skyward, the inevitable collapse to embers. Perhaps this fire-lust foretold the day our family would snap like sparks swirling and drifting away.

It Might Have Happened Like This

My 10-year-old brother is drawing cartoons at the round, wooden kitchen table. I smile at his frowning concentration, the deft way he outlines and shades—summoning a snout, a tail, a raised eyebrow, from the tips of his pencils. Our mom is at work and being twenty-two I'm the designated adult in the room—the room that smells of sour feet and the slightly burned mac and cheese he made for his third snack since lunch. I know he should get out of the house into the cut-grass-fragrant air of summer, and I could use some alone time. I open the fridge, see that he's drunk all but a splash of the milk—no doubt straight from the carton.

"Hey li'l bro, what about a walk to the store?" I say, tousling his mess of blonde hair, the tangles catching between my fingers.

He shrugs, still frowning. *"I'm busy."*

I palm him a five-dollar bill, tell him he can get a doughnut. He looks up, surprised. A grin materializes. He grips the money and saunters out the door, hands in his pockets. I call out, "*Don't do anything I wouldn't do!"* and he gives me a thumbs up over his shoulder.

We live three blocks from a cut-through street and sirens blast their way from highway to main drag morning and night, but this time there's urgency in the rising whine and abrupt stop. My brain calibrates the distance and time my brother's been gone, then telegraphs *run like hell* to my nervous system. I hurtle down the driveway, across two streets and down a third to where an ambulance flashes red, police cars angled to provide cover. There's a smallish form on the ground. Head on the curb. EMTs hovering. Blood in the gutter. Not a river but enough to make my stomach lurch. Nearing the scene, I hear the sing-song of his child's voice spiked with a man's salty language. My brother is kicking at the air, at the EMTs. Keening a stream of swears. *He's in shock,* I think. I hurl the words, *"I can help!"*

"Are you a doctor?"

"His sister."

They step back, offering no resistance as I drop to the sidewalk and tell my brother, *"I'm here now. It's gonna be OK. But you gotta cool it so I can ride in the ambulance with you."*

The kicking and cursing stop and just like that he's limp, resigned. They stretcher him. Load him. Bandage and monitor him. Inside the ambulance, the dome light throws bleak shadows. I hold my brother's hand, hoping to hold him together. Once we're moving, the EMTs tell me he was walking on the edge of the curb and slipped off just as a small pickup truck approached. The driver unable to stop in time.

In the ER, bleeping machines sow fresh panic. Smells of alcohol, antiseptic, rubber. Voices drifting through blue surgical masks and eyes peering out beneath clownish shower caps. The doctors allow me to stay long enough to calm him, so they can get a line in his arm. He drifts, eyes droop. They slide a tube into his nose, tell me to leave. Promise to keep me updated.

I slump to the waiting room. Collapsing into an orange leatherette chair I pull my thin jacket across my chest against the chill pulsing from the ceiling vent. The room throbs with artificial light and I stare at the too-loud TV on the wall. The blonde newscaster is cheerful, eyes flashing as she announces death tolls, earthquakes, air raids, tsunamis. I'm overcome by nausea, try to slow my breathing. Sitting nearby is a mother with her hand on a stroller, her little boy fluttering the baby's lips with his finger. I wonder who they're waiting for. I lower my head so they won't see the tears that gush unexpectedly.

After an eon, the tired-eyed doctor—with his barely-more-than peach-fuzz face—approaches. He taps my shoulder with latexed fingertips like I might infect him. Announces that my brother will *live*. He's going for x-rays, CAT scan, blood work and cast. Later I can visit him in the ICU where he'll stay *for quite some time*. The doctor leaves in a cloud of green scrubs and rubber gloves. Matching clown cap and slippers.

In a minute I'll go out to the courtyard where people in wheelchairs eat turkey and cheese sandwiches and dodge pollen-laden bees. I'll call Mom but not say, *I should never have let him walk alone on a busy street.* Not say, *you should've been home.* Not say, *how did everything get so messed up?* Instead I'll tell her *There was an accident, Mom. But it's gonna be OK.*

It might have happened like that.

But maybe I smile at my brother who's drawing cartoons, his brow tight with concentration and when I tousle his mess of blonde hair, the tangles catch between my fingers. Maybe when I say, *"Hey bro, take a break. Let's go get some milk and doughnuts,"* he looks up surprised, a grin materializing and we drive to the store in my rust-pocked gray VW Bug—five-dollar bill damp in my pocket, the cut-grass fragrance of summer fluttering into the car, my brother's hand trailing a little too far out the window.

Strawberry Blonde

When Timmy invited me over wearing that crisp, white shirt, sleeves rolled up, smelling like Irish Spring, we'd sit on his bed with the plaid comforter, arms barely brushing, listening to Beatles LPs. Homework optional. My skin prickled when we listened to Something In the Way. I was sure he felt the same.

We'd been friends since long before the tall eighth-grader sashayed into our midst, tossing her persimmon curls. Even when I saw them sharing glances across the classroom, I knew it was me he wanted, just had to overcome his shyness. She sure was hard to ignore, though.

Blue

The cutest kid in sixth grade, with his freckled face and aquamarine eyes, asked *me* to meet him at midnight on his front porch, when no one else would be around.

10:30 pm exactly. Snores and snorts from my parents' room down the hall. Thank God they sleep early. For another whole hour I have to lie in my bed quiet as a lizard, listening to my folding travel clock *tick, tick, tick*. I'm wide awake since I guzzled a can of Coke before bed and I can almost feel him squeezing my hand, asking me to go steady, giving me a ring he made from bark with his own double-jointed fingers. I saw him stripping wood with a pen knife, twisting it into a voodoo doll after a game of spin-the bottle under the mango tree in the overgrown lot that's full of three-foot grasses and three-inch grasshoppers that stick to your pants like leeches. He gave the doll to Chrissie for being the best kisser, and my cheeks got hot thinking how Chrissie cheated on her math test by looking at my paper and then got *me* in trouble. *Well, haha Chrissie. If you could only see me now.*

11:30 pm. I imagine his peanut-butter-and-jelly breath on my face when he says *thanks for coming*, his smile pinching a dimple into his left cheek. I pull on the rainbow-colored t-shirt and jean short-shorts I hid under the bed so mom wouldn't see them, sneak down the corridor and downstairs on tabby-cat feet, scared they'll hear my heart that's thumping like a tom-tom. I slip out the back door. *Humid.* It's always humid in West Palm. I smell Hibiscus flowers, chlorine from the neighbor's pool. Something shrieks, and hairs I didn't know I had stand up on my neck. *Just an owl,* I realize when its wings slap the Spanish moss that hangs down from the trees, upside-down ghouls in the darkness.

11:44 pm. South Olive is usually pretty busy, but mostly quiet on weeknights like now. Still, I stay towards the edge of the sidewalk closest to houses. It should only be ten minutes, if I run. But I'd stink of sweat by the time I got there, so I fast walk instead, wishing I'd snuck some of mom's deodorant. Wishing my heart would settle down. With only five more blocks to go, headlights flash right at me from a side street. I jump behind a palm tree, sure the driver saw me. What if he kidnaps me, chops me up and dumps my pieces in the Everglades for the alligators, like some kids at school swear they heard on the news. But the car passes and I wait for the red taillights to disappear and my fingers to stop throbbing before I slow-trot the rest of the way.

When I get to his street, it's black as tar on the beach after an oil spill. No porch lights, no street lights, just a firefly sparking, sparking. Finally, I find number Twenty-Seven, tiptoe up to the empty porch, thinking I'm either too early or too late. My Timex says 11:58, so I slide down, lean against the railing, tell my breath to *slow down*, rub my underarms and wipe the sweat off on my shorts.

12:01 am. There's a *shush shush*-ing next to the porch and I pull my knees up to my chest. *Is it him?* But it's followed by the yowl of a "horny tom cat," like my stepdad says when he thinks I can't hear.

12:06 am

12:11 am. The air feels cooler now and my skin is clammy. My heartbeat is back to dull thumps and my belly is achy.

12:15 am

12:18 am. Did he forget? Maybe he mixed up the day. Or couldn't stay awake the way I did. Maybe he *is* awake, grinning like he thinks he's the coolest kid in town.

12:21 am. I ghost-walk back to the street, the night air smelling nasty now, like rotten water or eggs. The tree frogs and crickets are so loud, it sounds like they're laughing. What will I do when I see him in class? Act like everything is fine, like I didn't really run through the dark night for the chance to look into those cool blue eyes at all, that I'm not the kind of girl who would ever fall for something like that.

Too Late

Our little eleventh-grade clique was something of a phenomenon at our high school. Probably had at least something to do with beating the odds and having *seven* carrot tops in the same grade. We'd coordinate our outfits and hair every morning, and discuss activities—like when to go for practice swims at the community pool, whose musty smell always seemed to prevail over chlorine. We'd rehearse what to say when Hy showed up for lifeguard duty, because, let's face it, Hy was a *god.* You'll probably guess this all happened way before #metoo and PC-ness when I tell you we delighted in calling ourselves the *nymphettes.*

One day, we skipped French class and walked down to the five-and-dime to buy seven barrettes with fake carnations—five yellow and two white—to clip into our copper hair. We'd already saved up our allowances to buy the most revealing tank suits you could find at Sears—which wasn't saying much—so we bought a size too small to emphasize our pale, burgeoning bodies.

On that gloomy Friday afternoon, we went to the rec center close to closing time, so we'd be the only swimmers. We strutted past the lifeguard chair on our way to the water, vying to capture Hy's gaze, but of course he ignored us. Even when Daphne eyed the bump in his Speedo and said, "You look good in purple, Hy," he kept his attention on his beefcake magazine.

As we slipped into the water, Cleo slapped Daphne's rear.

"It's so *obvious* he's a homo."

Daphne flipped a blaze of orange hair over her shoulder. "Do I *look* like I care? He's still a hunk."

We were splashing around and giggling, when Mae went in for the kill. "Oh *no!*" she said, trying to sound all bougie, removing the string of plastic beads from around her neck, 'I'm still wearing my pearls. Hy won't you be a sweetie and hold onto these for me?"

Hy sighed, but obligingly knelt down poolside to receive Mae's plainly fake offering. Taking advantage of his momentary imbalance, Mel reached up to stroke his muscular forearm, then yanked him forward into the pool where he landed with a great *plunk* and splash. The seven of us crowded over and around him, shrieking in delight. We swarmed and thrashed like a school of orange and white giant Koi at feeding time, kicking each other and sending up geysers of moss-green water. Now that we'd trapped him, we whispered to one another what we wanted to do with him. *Pull down his trunks! You hold him, I'll kiss him! Where'd he go, though?*

As abruptly as we'd begun our shenanigans, we halted, a hush descending over the dank pool like dusk and we backed away from each other until we formed a ring and the water settled. Mae began to whimper and Daphne slit her eyes. "Too late to clutch at your pearls, missy."

We all stared into the murk, some of us holding our breaths, until we made out Hy's rippling, half-submerged form. At first there was astonishment, even triumph on our faces, as if we'd discovered new power in mortality and we circled in closer, contemplating his beauty until reality summoned us toward the inevitable.

Saturdays At the Souk

Since Fatma and Zaineb turned fourteen, their mother let them go to the market alone. They knew Mama wanted to rest before making a big lamb and vegetable tagine for dinner and it was a chance for them to slip away from Baba's rules, *Stop hanging over the veranda railing, no TV until homework is done*, and from Mama's constant demands for help in the kitchen. The Souk was a coveted escape. Strangers pressed into crowded spaces yelling and bargaining in Arabic, French, Spanish, Berber, the shouts of the shopkeepers, "Cucumbers the size of babies' fingers!" "The freshest sesame cookies in town!" The twins let their scarves slide back on their heads, navigating the narrow passageways steeped in aromas of cinnamon, cumin, roasting nuts, a waft of donkey dung. Between stops at the butcher, greengrocer, and tea parlor they walked arm-in-arm, giggling when they passed beautiful boys in long dishdashes and shibshib sandals, widening their black-lashed eyes, letting their glances trail as long as they dared. On the way out, there was that guy with the camera, the one who wore his tight shirt open, showing his chest, who said they looked like models, wanted to photograph them in his studio. His name was Talal. He was a professional. Fatma smiled at him, but Zaynab poked her ribs, said let's go! and they ran laughing and tripping past him toward the shelter of home. His husky voice trailed after them. I'm here every Saturday, beautiful girls! Every Saturday.

In Alien Territory

As a little girl, it was usually about her refusing to put on a proper dress to greet the aunt (B.O.) and the uncle (bad teeth) who'd pick her up, kiss both cheeks, her mother giving her the look when she winced, tried to pull away.

At thirteen, her parents said she'd end up no good, with her incessant drawing and humming. She should be studying the "5 Rs" (wasn't it 3?) and practicing violin. Guitar was a no-go, so she'd learned in secret with her first boyfriend, Craig, who was twelve and half her height, but smelled like a sea breeze, knew how to kiss without slobbering. His parents let them study in his vaulted, sawdust-smelling attic room, never suspecting they were up to all that guitar-playing and smooching.

Later, she dreamed of art school. Pops was thinking doctor or lawyer, something shiny and presentable. So, she went where you could study whatever and your parents wouldn't know because you didn't have to declare a major until the end of Junior year. Once she graduated, they'd give up because she'd be an adult. Could drink in a bar, fight in a war, sleep with whomever she chose. Ruin her life in exactly the way she wanted. Or not.

She got her BFA in visual arts, told the 'rents it was pre-med, bought time saying her advisor advised her to take off a year before med school. Street art was her passion, and she admired Banksy and Shepard Fairey, but her true role models were the gritty graffiti artists who tagged subway cars, bridges, and abandoned buildings in the Bronx.

She waitressed at an upscale hamburger establishment, where you couldn't just get an f-ing burger. There were patties with bacon jam and *bleu* cheese, mushrooms and shallots, fire-roasted peppers and jalapeno mayonnaise, portobello and sage burgers, 75 different international beers on tap. But the tips were good and she had her own studio apartment in a rickety walk-up with a clothes line on the porch, a little yard where her neighbors let their dog out to poop. And she met Alfie, a bassist in a jazz band who taught music lessons and toured. Got by. Saturdays they both volunteered at a food coop, where they got a 15% discount, swapped vegan recipes, made a date to cook a Jamaican *Ital* stew, even making their own coconut milk from whole coconuts. She painted to his music, he composed riffs based on her graffiti-inspired drawings.

In a fever of optimism, she took Alfie home to meet her parents, but they refused to talk to him except obliquely. *So, when is that person getting a real job?* As if he wasn't sitting next to them on the mauve settee. That was it. She pulled Alfie out of the house, saying *at least we tried.* Next day she broke her lease, took her drawing supplies and guitar, and moved in with Alfie in his dank basement apartment that smelled of weed, onions and Alfie.

Banging Pots and Pans

An American in South Lebanon

My fiancé's mother looks me up and down, purses her lips, walks away, slippers tch-tch-ing. I hear her mutter, *You send your sons off to study in America and this is what happens.*

"Don't worry," my fiancé whispers, waggling his unibrow, "once she gets to know you, she'll love you."

"Inshallah," I say. Though I appreciate his optimism and the 'stache with a gap in the middle, like the inverse of the unibrow, I know his mother has his sassy cousin with the green eyes in mind for him. I'm not the right ethnicity, right religion. I don't even *have* a religion for that matter. And we're living in sin. She's told everyone we're married. She'll have no scandal in her household. As a nurse-midwife she's used to being in charge—has no patience for nonsense. I can see there'll be no time for jet-lag or romance. Until we get our own place I'd best roll up my sleeves and start figuring things out.

Turkish Coffee

Open the jar of freshly ground dark coffee beans and breathe in the earthy aroma singing with the brightness of ground cardamom. Boil water in the long-handled pot whose lid looks like a beret with a wooden knob. Remove from the heat. Tip in five generous teaspoonfuls. Not too much. Not too little. Hold over the flame and lift up when the foam rises. Lower it back down until the foam rises again. Repeat until it settles but there's still a skim of foam on top. Pour.

6:30 Saturday Morning

Every pot and pan in the house has come alive and is banging about in the kitchen. She's up and now everyone else is too. My fiancé kicks at the sheet. It's August and heat and humidity cling to us though the sun has barely crept above the Mediterranean whose sweet, briny breath reaches across the few blocks to his mother's building to greet us. I start to get up. "Stay," he says hopefully, looping his slippery, sweat-slicked arms around my waist. "Don't let her guilt-trip you."

I kiss his smooth chest that tastes as salty as the sea. Yesterday I overheard her telling him, "This is all wrong. All wrong."

"I have to at least *try* to win her over," I say slipping from his damp embrace. He gives up, rolls onto his back. The pots and pans are sounding more like war drums now.

By the time I wash and dress she's sitting with a huge metal platter on her lap, house dress hiked up above her chubby knees. The platter is piled with zucchini and eggplant. She fixes her dark, intelligent eyes on mine, beaming a silent warning, but she lets me kiss her on both cheeks.

Stuffed Kuusa and Baytinjan

Always pick the smallest. Wash and cut off the tops. Core carefully to remove most of the pulp without poking through the delicate skin. And, yalla, don't dilly-dally—there's much to be done. Save the first cork-like cored bit from each one to seal in the filling. Mix ground beef or lamb, rice, and seven-spice mix in a large bowl. Stuff the mixture loosely into the vegetables. "Cork" them and place in a large pot. Boil in tomato sauce and broth seasoned with salt and a little more spice mix. They should be slightly firm but always tender.

Morning Coffee Break

I've memorized the routine after a few days: when the neighbors in the building come for coffee mid-morning—while there's still a cooling breeze out on the balcony—it's ok to greet them in a house dress. The coffee is served on the inlaid Syrian tray, with tiny spoons for sugar and handle-less cups that fit snugly in your palm—the everyday ones with the red and green fern-and-flower design. If there's a special guest, you should dress nicely, offer the coffee in gold-patterned demitasse cups, stir in the sugar for them. If a male visitor arrives, she'll put on her head scarf before he enters. If a woman comes to her clinic in labor, she'll go downstairs to get her settled, give her something to take the edge off. She'll instruct the husband to go wait in the waiting area and not tell her how to do her job.

On such days she'll tell me *Be a good girl and get breakfast ready*, frown when she says *good girl,* as if she's sure I won't be. I'm transported back to kindergarten.

Mana'ish

Roll out the dough into rounds. Stir fresh olive oil into the wild thyme-sumac-sesame-seed blend. Spread onto some of the dough. The others take a little oil and Akawi cheese. Cover them with a cloth and run them down to the bread bakery. They'll bring them back nicely baked. Serve with strong, sweet black tea and a plate of tiny cucumbers, mountain tomatoes, scallions, mint, olives and radishes.

A Place of Our Own

It's just over a month when we find an apartment in Beirut.

It feels like a lifetime and we're not even married yet. At the door she sets down three grocery sacks for us to take with us. Oranges from her brother's grove. Cherries. Loquats. Watermelon. A tray of *kibbeh*, a pan of fragrantly garlicky chicken and potatoes. A large jug of tart yogurt.

She kisses her son's cheeks. "Congratulations on the new flat. Don't stay away long, naughty boy."

We'll be living only an hour from her but there's a sadness in her eyes as if we're venturing far, far away. She turns to me with a mischievous half-smile, pinches my arm. I jump and she says, "One day when you have children of your own, you'll understand. Take good care of my boy. And you," she says pointing a knobbed finger at her son, "take care of her too."

For Better, For Worse

I sat alone in the corner, while the other dancers strutted, swirled, stomped. I already danced myself sore, blistered, and exhausted six days a week for the benefit of those camera-happy tourists with their twangy accents and ill-fitting clothes, but the *damas* had wheedled and nagged until I agreed to show up for the Sunday wedding celebration. I wore my ruffled, red *traje de flamenca*, but I was as firm as a *Sandalo* striking the floor—there was no way I'd be performing.

And no fake smiles for the joyous couple on their special day either. The whole thing made me want to vanish in a crimson cloud. I'd only agreed so as to avoid the inevitable. Better to endure the twang of strings, stink of ripe armpits, bright lights and carnival colors than be at home with my fork-tongued husband now that I knew the truth of where he'd been spending all those long, hard nights. I longed to slip away—from them, from him. To embrace solitude, darkness, and most of all, quiet. Rest my throbbing calves and undulating brain, alone in my saggy bed, far from all that joy.

Red Lava

He said he was living in his parents' one-room garage until he could afford his own place, that he'd decked it out like a scene from a 70s movie: red lava lamp in the corner, posters of trippy fractals on the walls, a silkscreen of Hendrix on the ceiling, shag rug on the floor in front of the mattress that was covered with an Indian bedspread. *Come see for yourself,* he said.

She was surprised to see it was a standalone structure—a squat concrete cube engulfed by ivy and surrounded by a tangle of dandelions, crabgrass and sunflowers, a cracked birdbath at one end of the lot. Charming in a shabby sort of way. He rolled up the corrugated garage gate to let her in, then lowered and locked it, saying that way his parents couldn't get in. They didn't like it when he brought girls there, especially his father—a real bastard of an ex-marine, he said. No point taking chances. It felt strange being locked in with this person she hardly knew, but the place was tidy and lying on his bed kissing in the glow of the lava lamp, the smell of sandalwood incense wafting around them in his hippie hideaway, she felt daring but safe, intrigued to be suspended in this windowless box, and after a while she had the disorienting sense that it might still be light outside or could be dark. She didn't know and didn't care, especially once they'd downed a couple of tequila shots and the room started to tilt around her.

She wasn't used to hard liquor and her grip on reality was slipping and that's when something started to shift. Him groping her body aggressively, when he'd been all tender and easy-going a few minutes before. Him pinning her hands against the bed and pressing harder when she resisted. Her breath coming faster, not from excitement but something more like panic, and maybe he'd think it meant she was into it and she said *slow down* but he laughed, downed another shot or two, jammed his knee between her legs, saying how hot she was and not listening to her saying *stop, I'm not ready for this,* and the room spinning and the red glow from the lava lamp menacing instead of romantic now as she searched for a way out but found none and she scanned and scanned until her eyes locked on a steel flashlight on the bedside table. She wondered if there really were any parents, or if he'd made them up so she'd be trusting enough to walk willingly into his lair, like a fox following the scent of food into a trap that snaps shut, the animal realizing its mistake a moment too late as its leg is crushed by the jagged metal teeth.

And when he raised up off her to get a fifth or sixth shot, his knees still on her thighs she asked *where's the bathroom* and he said she could use the bucket in the corner if she really had to and she thought of him flirting from the next booth at the diner when they first met, his easy smile and musky scent when he asked if he could join her, how she even found his Wolverine-style sideburns oddly attractive, and she'd laughed and said sure. He'd said he was a line cook there, that Tuesday was his day off, and after that they started meeting up for coffee Tuesday mornings, the warm smells of eggs and toast and bacon swirling around them, and she got so comfortable with him that going to his "pad" seemed like no big deal, but now she was thinking maybe that line about being a line cook was a lie even though he knew all the waitresses by name. Maybe he wasn't anything he claimed and maybe when he was done with her, he'd dispose of her behind a dumpster, leave her to die.

And maybe he had bet on her being meek and fragile and compliant and didn't expect her to grab that flashlight instead of peeing in the paint bucket with him in the same room and maybe he was too hammered to notice when she was behind him lifting and then bringing the weight of it down on his head, maybe he hadn't thought her capable of such a thing—at the diner he'd said how sweet she was—and maybe he realized too late that he'd got it wrong, and a little sound, a surprised exhale, came out from between his parted lips as he slumped forward, a rivulet of red spreading onto the Indian quilt the same color as the red blobs in the lava lamp. And she kept that flashlight raised because now she had to slide her other hand inside his pocket to fish out the key and maybe he'd suddenly whirl around and grab her arm like Godzilla rising up enraged and slam her against the wall to finish her off. But her hand made it into the pocket and out again, the key gripped between trembling fingers and she had to turn her back to him in order to get the key in the lock and turn it and raise the gate and escape into the fresh air of the night and run and run in the fine misting drizzle and try not to think about the gossipy waitresses or her fingerprints under a blue light all over his body and the bed and the flashlight she'd dropped at the last minute.

Snake. Taos New Mexico

After he broke the restraining order for the second time, she put two suitcases and her little boy in the old Chevy and started driving west. To anywhere. The farther the better. Wherever they'd be anonymous. She'd been to Santa Fe once as a teenager, was smitten by that land so ancient it laughed at history, the air that smelled of brush smoke and sage, sun that reached out and embraced you without having to struggle through smog. She told the boy it was a special adventure just for the two of them. She'd figure it out as she went along.

She drove, engine straining to its limit, through the shrub-mottled Sangre de Cristo range, past striated mesas, the deep ravine of the Rio Grande plunging low to the left. The road wound gently at first, then spiraled tighter around the contours of the mountain until the switchbacks reversed so sharply she imagined hurtling into the dusty abyss if the brakes didn't hold or she was distracted by the child. All the while, she sang to the boy, who cried for his daddy, cried for his friends, cried for his bed and the wild animal mobile that hung from the ceiling. He finally slept suckling his fingers, as the soft adobe contours of the town, cradled in the valley just below, spirited into view. *Taos.* It seemed to beckon as if expecting them.

In her panic to leave, she'd hurled his blankie, Elmo slippers, and Tigger, into the bag, but somehow missed *Goodnight Moon.* So, once they found a motel, she promised that after breakfast the next morning they'd drive to the patchouli-scented bookstore on the Plaza to get a new one.

He wailed that he wanted *his* copy but was mollified by promises of chocolate ice cream. She would have promised him a real tiger just to get through the day, but ice cream and a book that sang to him like a lullaby had worked this time.

As they headed back to the car from the store, he clutched the shiny new book in one hand, fingers the size of cornichons gripping her thumb, his soft hair waving like feathergrass, plump legs pumping to keep up. Piñon jays squawked overhead in the electric-blue sky, the air so fresh and clear she felt it healing her with every breath. Everything stood out vividly in the sparse, clear atmosphere—cinnamon-hued houses, a turquoise gate, arnica, aloe plants, the pink of bitter dogbane flowers—all seemed to be lit from within.

Something caught the boy's attention and he dropped her finger and pointed. A brown and black and yellow snake ribboned sleekly, rapidly, across the parking lot in front of them.

Look Mama, 'nake.

He squatted to admire the creature that looked as if someone had woven strands of rope into a glossy braid, and released it to wind and unwind its way to safety.

At the same moment, two men in cowboy hats and heeled boots ambled toward their Ford pickup, all cocksure male swagger. They laughed, jumped into the vehicle, backed up fast towards the snake. She yanked the boy's arm and he yelped, looked up at the men who were craning their necks backwards out the window for better aim. He pointed and yelled in his small voice *'nake! 'nake!* to warn the men as the snake disappeared under their tires.

He tugged at her shirt. *Why did they do that, Mama?*

She lied that they hadn't noticed, pulled him close to her side as the gears grated, the truck lurching into first, hurtling forward to finish the job. She knuckled her hands into fists, thinking how she'd driven two thousand miles to shelter the boy from the rage in his father, a rage that had passed through generations, like the stone-gray eyes and cleft chin that were so charming on the little one.

The boy kept saying *why Mama? why did they do that?* She eyed a rock on the curb beside her, calculated that the truck was within striking distance. She squatted down, curled her fingers around it, but the boy started wailing, reached his arm out stiffly toward the snake, as the vehicle sped out of range, wheels screeching, the stench of hot rubber clouding the air.

She let the rock slip out of her hand, drew him up into her arms, saying *I don't know baby, I don't know*, turned her body away from the oozing snake so he wouldn't see.

A Changed Man

It was a year since Clementine had given Luke the boot. He was always crooning "Oh my darling, oh my darling," air banjo on his knee, but he never cooked a meal, never put a dollar towards rent. So, she'd rolled his duct-taped suitcase out the door, taken back his key.

Her roomie, Anna, though, kept whining she missed having a man in the house and *she* didn't mind his lazy ass, so when they hosted a potluck and Luke sauntered in uninvited, carrying a caramel-brown roast chicken ringed with delicate potatoes and carrots, Clementine side-eyed Anna. All the same, she'd licked her soy-ginger-coated fingers clean, one by one, and Luke had raised an eyebrow, strummed those strings.

A few weeks later, Clementine slumped into the kitchen, thwacked that brass key down onto the counter, where Anna sat munching on a slice of cold cheese pizza. "But he really *seemed* like a changed man," she said.

Anna mimed Luke carrying the platter. "Must have been that Trojan Chicken."

Between Springtime and Night

She stood on the tiny patch of grass clutching a cluster of flowers—pale pastels. All the color she could bear. For so long it had seemed to her that every day was a choice though most days she didn't have strength to choose. She'd seen that abyss up close, that cavernous mouth of dark that threatened to devour her, devour everything light and good. She almost wished it would, sucking away her grief as well. But then it settled—this thick, solid presence inside her, and she lost track of the days since he left, gliding through time on the rituals of the living—waking to the sage smoke smell of him still clinging to the soft quilt, watching the steam from her morning tea rise and writhe before vanishing in the sun. At the keyboard, her fingers performed their perfunctory duties as if no thought were required, obediently producing figures—looping black on a sheet of white, figures that might once have made sense to her, seemed profound, even. Sometimes, when the bright was too much, flickering and flashing as if mocking her despair, she'd pull the shades, only realize night was coming when sadness blanketed the numbness of day.

The damp grass is cool between her toes now as she gazes at the darkness that once held her in thrall. A tremble of warm air fragrant with hyacinth is at her back, ruffling her skirt, lifting her hair. Even now she hesitates between springtime and night, gripping those pale flowers.

As In Life

My mother thrived on attention, itched for drama. She left my quiet, reclusive father because of it. On a Friday she died. Sunday an epic rainstorm flooded Mystic Valley Parkway in our town and people rowed in little boats to higher ground. Even in death she was impossible to ignore.

Aurora

Anna reached into her pocket. How could she have forgotten her cell phone in the car? When it was cold like this, lots of powdery snow from last week's storm, she could go all day seeing no one, like today.

Anna had been hiking in the mountains for years, had started when she and Brett lived high in the Sangre de Cristo mountains. She'd spend the day up there whenever she needed solitude, or they'd had one of those spats that seemed to materialize from nothing—a pile of dirty clothes in the bedroom, a careless interruption. The hikes always seemed to help, the few hours apart enough to "press the reset button" as Brett would say. By the time she returned he'd had enough time to worry—but not enough to be alarmed. She'd arrive cold and fever-cheeked and he'd lure her to the bedroom with hot cocoa and they'd make grateful love under the moose-and-snowy-pine patterned quilt.

She thought of those days now as the sun dipped lower. They'd lived in New Hampshire for seven years, but she'd never really made her peace with the trails in the Whites, some part of her resisting, longing for the familiar bird calls, radiant sun and dry-clay air of northern New Mexico. Back home, she'd know which ridge to follow until it descended into the valley.

But Brett's work had brought them here and she did like the padded feel of pine needles underfoot, the leaves in autumn that looked like flames leaping up from the ravine.

Over the years, they'd adjusted expectations, each letting in enough of the bad habits of the other that their differences began to blur. Still, she usually preferred venturing out alone. Since they both worked at home, it gave her time to think, visualizing her next project without distraction.

But with the air rapidly cooling, the sun's angle declining, she wished he was with her. He was a red fox out there, bounding confidently from rock to rock, never losing his way. Anna had been thinking of the painting she was working on, that can of turpentine she needed, had unconsciously avoided icy segments of the path in what seemed like minor diversions. So where was the trail? What about that last slick patch she'd sidestepped near the overhanging boulder? How could it not be obvious?

It was the tingling down her neck, though, her stomach querling around itself, that finally made her accept she was lost. She knew she could freeze out here and no-one would find her until daylight. The temperature could easily drop into the teens or single digits without the still-strong December sun to warm the air. *I should've headed back way sooner. Stupid, stupid.*

Her breaths came quick and shallow, lightheadedness forcing her to catch her balance against a tree. *Get a grip, Anna. If you faint, you're fucked.* She drew long breaths into her abdomen, tried to clear her mind of everything except making a plan. She scouted around for any enclosure where she could shelter. But even inside a cave she might not survive the night.

Suddenly, she remembered their wilderness trip to Northern Maine where a group of campers learned from their Canadian guide how to make a quinzie by hollowing out a tent-like mound of snow. It wasn't quite as sturdy as an igloo, but still worked, and they'd slept inside overnight. But they'd had shovels and picks, arctic-rated sleeping bags. All Anna had was a metal water bottle and her heavily-gloved hands, so she set about plastering snow onto a small mound to increase its size to where she hoped it would hold her scrunched body. Trickiest would be coring it, *like carving a pumpkin,* the guide had said. Without tools, though, it felt much harder than that. She wasn't even sure it was possible, but she hacked away with the lid-end of the canteen, using her fingers like ice picks as the sky turned a mottled gray-pink. She remembered that you were supposed to jam sticks into the mound a couple feet deep so you wouldn't poke through the sides. *No time now,* she thought, *keep digging.*

Eventually she'd dug a crude, lumpy cavern and her fingers had no feeling left in them. She checked her watch. *7:23*. It had taken hours. She hurriedly gathered leaves and pine needles, piled them inside. That would have to do. She'd need her remaining energy to get through the night. Anna used her pee funnel before climbing in, looked up to the indigo sky crowded with stars. A faint milky curtain pulsed across her vision. Disoriented, she squeezed her eyes shut and looked again, before understanding. *Northern lights!* Not the throbbing purple and green type she'd seen in videos, but no less magical in their ghostly swaying. She wished Brett was there. He was always saying how one day he'd find a way to see the aurora borealis.

Anna eased herself in through the tiny opening, knowing if it broke, she wouldn't have another chance. She huddled inside her tiny den, pulled off her soaked gloves, the material scraping like knives against her half-frozen skin, fingers quobbled from wetness. She removed her scarf and wound it around her head, neck and hands, blowing warm air slowly, slowly onto her fingers. She remembered the energy bar in her pocket, would eat it as soon as she could still her shaking. She thought how relieved Brett used to be when she made it home from her wanderings, wondered what he'd be thinking now. Was he looking for her? She strained to hear in case he was calling through the gelid air—*Anna*—*Anna*—but heard nothing except the wind's tuneless song, the hushed silence of the cave walls, the *shush-shush* of her down coat as she pulled her knees up. She breathed in the sweet resin of her pine bed, pictured the aurora ribboning silently outside, feared sleep but was unable to resist it.

The Breach

She'd long since despaired of his return, but the press of his rough fingers on the small of her back, the smoke and salt of his lips, were imprinted in her psyche despite all efforts at forgetting. She'd waited for the groan of the fickle doorbell until waiting became a humiliation and her thoughts turned bitter in the hard loneliness of her bed. She vowed if he ever reappeared, he wouldn't make it past the threshold. But then there he was, lunch box in hand on that chilly autumn day, the smell of decaying leaves and wood fire in the air, as if he'd just been off working at the construction site and was home for supper. And just like that she was back in his arms, gnawing at his mouth, the lunch box dropping with a metallic clank, all the questions and mysteries between them seething in their embrace.

Three-Legged

What would've happened if we'd never met—only shared a glance and a smile across a packed auditorium, the fresh lacquer smell of the stage mingling with stale cigarette smoke? No locking hands across the ocean, no dewy-haired bairns. I might always have wondered how it would feel to touch your smooth chest slick with sweat in the still night, to hear your voice thrumming with want, feel your body vine around mine, fall into sleep already yearning for more.

What would've happened if we'd met a decade later on a ferry steaming across the Sound, diesel smoke descending in wafts, both of us hanging over the railing to feel the salt spray envelop us, the blast of the air horn making us both jump, laugh, at the same moment thinking, do I know you from somewhere?

What would've happened if we had met those many years ago—in a dim oak-paneled bar that smelled of whiskey and onions, Let's Go Crazy pumping through the speakers and we'd looked at each other with something like recognition and ended up in your saggy bed talking all night, our bodies glistening in the light of a humming street light outside your window, your three-legged rescue cat purring between us, kneading the sweaty sheets—but when I told you about him, your trusting gaze hardened to glass?

A Breath of Fresh Air

Cloris and her friends were dancing, plucking oranges and thinking about love when Zeph snuck up on her as if from left field. Her companions were so distracted with their frolicking they didn't even notice him grabbing her waist as if he owned her, then turning all gentle and sweet when they noticed him.

Cloris knew he was the type who had to prove he could have any woman he wanted even if she was his brother Boris' girlfriend. He loved the challenge, didn't care how many hearts he broke in the process.

Everyone but Cloris was just happy to see Zeph cheerful after months of the blues, wallowing in his seasonal affective disorder. He was a breath of fresh air, they said, made everything seem right with the world again.

After that, whenever Zeph showed up, Cloris' girlfriends got all flirty and doe-eyed, made not-so subtle hints about how she should dump Boris for Zeph. After all, they said, Boris and Cloris just sounded all wrong. And Cloris had to admit to herself that she was getting sick of Boris' temper, how cold he could be at times. He was just the opposite of Zeph—loved everything about winter and grew sullen and distant when the snows melted and tender buds began to emerge.

In contrast, Zeph lavished attention on her, arms overflowing with heavenly-smelling hyacinth, lilacs and roses. He turned on the charm, wooing her patiently. The final blow was when Boris stormed off just because Cloris said how happy she was that winter was finally over. When Zeph showed up to comfort her, she finally relented. "I knew," Zeph said with that upside-down smile of his, "my persistence would bear fruit eventually. As will you and I," he added with a wink.

Cloris still wasn't sure she could trust Zeph, but with time she reconciled herself to occasionally sharing him with another girl or boy. After all, she knew she'd be the one soothing him and bringing him pomegranate juice when his S.A.D. got bad, that they'd always get through it together and rejoice in the bounty of their love.

Silence Is a Stranger

What we'd argued about seems beside the point. Mostly there was the sensation of my feet slipping on the shifting dune. A fall, a crash, a seemingly unbreachable silence. It took a death, a shared grief, to unravel it—our eyes meeting across a room filled with faceless mourners mollifying sadness with canapes, cake and wine. After that, it was almost easy. As if it had never even happened.

Heart In a Box

I pull the leaf from its box, edges slightly curled, heart-shaped core roseate, as I found it one year after you passed. Nestled in my palm, it beats with the secrets it conceals. And I'm left with all the questions that remained unspoken when you were alive yet can now only wonder about. Why you carried such sadness, shrank from hard truths, broke our family into a thousand bits. I replace the delicate heart in its tomb, hoping to quiet its urgent pulsing. You are free now, but what might you have revealed if I'd found the courage to ask?

Refuge

Rain is rat-a-tatting the windows and lightning jolts the sky hotter than the surface of the sun. I thrill to that wild music, fling open the door, breathe in smells of wet soil and rock. And I'm sixteen again, stealing out of my stepfather's house to the refuge of bellowing skies, bare arms puckering. I bound barefoot and ecstatic through empty streets, waterfalls sluicing down my back, and when thunder resounds through my drenched body, I dance harder, spinning like a dervish. Now my small, fearless dog is beside me on my own porch—all pointed ears, hackles and erect tail—sounding her fierce warning barks. Utterly wise in the ways of the world, I am sure she is telling me, *get inside, fool, it's perfectly safe in there.*

I'm More My Father Than My Mother

Sturdy. Steady. More Ukraine than UK. Yet in a shop window I see her eyes. Sometimes feel her angst, dread, the fear of aging, undesirability, loss. Like it's my own. Then too there's the pleasure of walks in woods, gaping into tide pools at tiny, translucent shrimp, feeling the suffering of people and animals like a knife in my gut. The rocking and clacking of trains taking me away. The give of dough under my hands, zing of cardamom, anise, ginger, the sensual feel of song in my throat. Still I always say, I'm more my father than my mother.

Thousand-Watt Smile

Sara nearly dropped the peeling tin box of Grandpa Teddy's things when she pulled out the yellowed, cracked, black and white of Grandma Bea sitting on the wheel hub of their '38 Chevy, chubby ankles crossed.

Sara was only sure the picture was her grandmother because of the distinctive contour that had been carved around where her head and upper body should have been. She didn't remember Bea, who'd died when Sara was barely two years old, so as a girl, whenever she'd visit Teddy, she'd ask to see the heart-shaped picture, the one with Bea wearing a beret over dark, wavy hair. The photograph was tucked into the corner of the mirror of the bureau Teddy shared with Bea for thirty years—the top two drawers hers, the bottom two his. Bea's smiling face shone out from behind Teddy's Old Spice aftershave, hair trimmer, and zippered shoe polish kit neatly arranged on the bureau top, a stack of accounting ledgers and a fountain pen off to one side. Bea's gold locket engraved with the letters "BL" hung from the mirror next to the picture.

"That's her 1000-watt smile," Teddy would say, holding the heart in his hands. "When she walked into a room, everyone looked up, men *and* women. She was a looker, my Bea, and as sweet as can *be,"* he'd say, chuckling at his own joke.

Sara had been told that her grandmother died of a heart attack, and when she was growing up, Teddy would pat her hand and say, "Take care of that ticker! It's the only one you got."

Now that Teddy was gone, Sara was going through his things before the house went on the market. Inside the eave closet that smelled of old wood and mouse droppings, she stared at this lost companion piece, a heart-shaped hole where Bea's smiling face should have been. A rusty paper clip held the "*Daily Sun*" article to the back of the photo. Sara's eyes were drawn first to the image of a stockier, more serious Bea than the one frozen in her imagination. Then to the headline:

"Local Grandmother Dies in Briarview Asylum Incident"

Sara crumpled onto Teddy's dusty steamer trunk with its brass latches and leather straps. She'd looked at the tidy, heart-shaped picture dozens of times, but seeing Bea's disembodied hands and feet against the old car, reading those cryptic words, reality seemed to slip like a wave receding beneath her feet. Bea was institutionalized? What did they do to her? Had Sara's mother known the truth? Sara tried to imagine the shame and anguish Teddy must have endured for the forty-five years after Bea left him all alone until his own death at just shy of a hundred; what it must have taken for her guileless grandfather to carry that carefully-constructed lie all those years and to pass it on to his granddaughter as smoothly as slipping the heart-shaped picture of Bea into her hands.

She-Wolf

Sara's dog, She-Wolf, lay with her legs in a triangle, vertex aimed at Tom. Snout aloft, she took in the aromas of last night's stew, overgrown basil from the window planter, Tom's ripe socks.

Tom shifted uncomfortably on the sway-backed couch. "I can't do this anymore," he said.

Sara lowered her book and blinked at him over her glasses, mind spinning like a flywheel. The pandemic year *had* put them both on edge. Too little space, too much togetherness.

She-Wolf was the only one happy with the arrangement. But all in all, Sara thought they were muddling along reasonably well.

"Do what? What this?"

"It's your dog."

She-Wolf's nimble nose twitched right, left, left, right.

"She-Wolf? What'd she do now? Pee on your pepper patch?"

The dog curled her tongue in a yawn, shimmied her legs forward into an even more acute angle. The sun skewed in through the window, casting half of Tom's face in shadow, a tragicomedy mask of emotion.

"It's so obvious she hates me. How do you not see it?"

"That's ridiculous, Tom. Example?"

"Like every time I play a sour note on the piano, I swear to God she winces."

Sara narrowed her eyes at the thought of Tom playing the same three Ragtime pieces over and over, never very well. Thought of how She-Wolf's pointy ears would flatten whenever she heard the squeak of car brakes or squawk of a blue jay outside the window.

"OK. What else?"

"I get no respect! She pulls away and growls when I try and pet her, leaves tooth marks on every pair of my shoes, but never touches yours, turns her tail to me and farts when I tell her to stop yapping."

Sara laughed. "Well, y'know, Shibas are super smart and independent, in addition to mad cute."

"Yeah—and alpha to the max. Always busting my balls."

"A good thing," Sara muttered, her words muted by the jackhammering and car horns from the street.

"What?"

"It's a good thing. Being alpha."

"Not when I disagree with something you say and she curls

her lip over her gum and it sticks there like a southern sheriff pulling his shirt up over his holster."

"Mmmm. Mm-hmmm. Tom?"

Tom didn't answer, just glowered at her.

Sara set her book down, pushed her glasses onto her head. It seemed so clear now, what had been half-hidden in the rhythm and din of everyday life, what lay right in front of her, but she hadn't wanted to see.

Chain of Fools

It's a sun-drenched cut-grass balmy-air day and I'm speeding down the street in a borrowed jalopy as Aretha wails *One of these mornings* on the radio hair tousling elbow out the window feeling strong when I see my boo with his Frank Zappa moustache and winning grin driving the other way and I wave *the chain is gonna break* and I laugh and my heart thumps *chain chain chain* and that's when I notice the concrete truck crossing from a side street in front of me and I pump the brakes like mom taught me to do but nothing happens and I turn the wheel hard and I'm parallel with the beast looming next to me its whirligig thing mixing concrete ready to pour and the road is narrowing and I'm pounding the horn *chain chain chain* but nothing comes out and I scream and I scream and the driver looks over and the "O" of his mouth is like the "O" of the concrete chute and he jams his brakes that Omigod work but now he's scowling and I'm squid-armed and quaking and now I can never say *thank you mister I'm still alive I'm still alive I'm still alive.*

Made For Walking

She drew them on one by one, found herself singing "*These Boots Are Made for Walking*" because they were. Made for marching right the hell out that door. They were masculine boots like the Marines wear, but with laces the papaya hue of puffin's feet—a little comical perhaps, but that's how they came and who gave a shit anymore anyway? She had allowed herself to be too tender, showing him the soft pink of herself too soon. Now she'd stride through life, one heavy foot in front of the other, no problem too great for this soldier. And if she felt herself start to sink, felt that old trickle of fear, she'd tuck her flower petal heart under her wing, pull on those boots and get walking.

Phantom Husband

Sara picked up the newspaper, held it at arm's length, then drew it closer, the pages trembling like a hummingbird between her hands. She peered at the man in the grainy photo—the bow tie, trench coat, one eyebrow raised, no wedding ring—tried to reconcile the image with the words.

> *Larry Joseph Bell, 57, of Lexington, Mass dies in Framingham crash…survived by wife, Ella and children Emma and Olivia.*

She scanned the room for her phone, got up too fast, blood whooshing from her head into her feet. Larry had left just days before, said he'd be back Tuesday. In their fourteen years of marriage he often went on the road for work and she hadn't given it a second thought. Now her thoughts ricocheted like a tennis ball. Maybe the paper got hold of a photo of the wrong Larry Joseph Bell. Or it was some sick hoax. No way he'd died. She would've been notified. And who the hell were Ella, Emma and Olivia?

Sara had long since stopped loving Larry. He was like a stranger to her and she'd always assumed he was having affairs. She'd only stayed because of their boys. She was glad they were at school now so she had time to think. She steadied herself against the vinyl-topped table, felt around until her fingers grazed the cracked face of her iPhone—the one she inherited from Larry when he upgraded. She pulled up *Favorites,* pressed *Phantom Husband*—her nickname for Larry that suddenly seemed less amusing. The call went straight to voicemail. Again she pressed.

Again, voicemail.

Larry had always claimed he had no living relatives, so she called her friend Sue, asked if John had seen him at the gym. He hadn't. She called everyone who might know something, but *nada.*

Heart thumping, Sara finally dialed Framingham police but the detective insisted they couldn't discuss "the case," that they were already in touch with his wife. When she said she *was* his wife, all she got was a "sorry Ma'am." She called the newspaper next, but the person who handled obits assured her they'd checked all the "facts," gotten the photo from *the wife.* Sara screamed, "I am the fucking wife!" slammed down the phone.

She studied the picture again, thought of all those sales trips and weekends away. How she'd wearied of him and his excuses, convinced herself she didn't care, was even relieved when he'd go on the road. But *this?*

Next morning, still dry-eyed and keeping silent for the moment, Sara dropped Greg and Tim at the middle school, growled onto I-95 in her sturdy old Subaru, exhaust and humid air skulking in through the open window. It hadn't been hard to find the address on the internet. Ninety minutes to Lexington. Ninety minutes of tortured thoughts. Her parents' anger when they learned she was seeing a man sixteen years her senior. How daring she'd felt at first. How they'd drifted. She pictured his face smashed crimson into the windshield, and panic flooded in. She gripped the wheel, forced away the image.

Sara gawped at the English tudor, with its ivy-shimmered chimney. Home to Ella, Emma, Olivia and—evidently—Larry. An emerald lawn hedged the path to the front door with its lion's-head knocker that broadcast its metallic message to the interior. Such a contrast to her own peeling duplex that listed slightly to one side. The woman who answered appeared to be around fifty—slim and pretty in spite of dark pouches under her eyes.

Sara apologized for showing up unannounced, said she was a relative of Larry's, hadn't been in touch recently and would Ella mind if she came in to talk? Ella hesitated, saying the funeral was Friday. There was still so much to do. Sara looked away, wondered if this was a mistake, but Ella touched her elbow, gestured for her to enter.

"Of course. Come in. I'm just a bit overwhelmed right now."

Sara promised to stay only a few minutes and the two women sat across the island from each other, sipping Earl Grey, its perfuminess assaulting Sara's tongue. Ella was very put-together—so unlike Sara in her shapeless sweatsuit. She wished she'd thought to pin up her hair, wear something nice.

"I can't believe he's gone," Ella said, eyes rimmed red. "After twenty-five years. Just—gone."

Sara eyed the photos on the counter—two identical young women in caps and gowns, flushed cheeks pressed together, wavy blonde hair flowing between them like a river.

"What'd he do for a living?"

"He was a pharma exec," Ella said, frowning puzzlement. "He was always travelling—but he was good to us." She glanced at the picture. "The twins are a wreck."

Sara sighed. "I don't know how else to say this, Ella, but he was my husband, too." Bewilderment shrouded Ella's face as Sara explained that Larry supposedly sold medical devices, that they'd managed, bought a fixer-upper, that she and the boys barely saw him and now she got why.

Sara ran her hand over the rough-textured cloth of the photo album she'd brought as proof of her life with Larry, slid it across the island. Ella took in each picture, her face twisted with grief and confusion. Larry and Sara at their wedding. At the playground with Tim and Greg.

"That's my Larry," Sara said, "and our boys." Ella snapped the album shut, stood abruptly. "I think you should go now. Please."

Sara sat in the car allowing the strangeness of it all to sink in, thought of poor Ella—doubly broken now. *You really got us, Lar. Who'd have thought you clever enough? Or rich enough. Hell, Ella and I could've been sister wives. I could totally see myself in that kitchen with the Viking stove, all that granite.*

She put the car in gear, headed back to her run-down digs and smart, handsome sons. *At least I got them out of the deal,* she thought and for the first time since reading the obituary, Sara wept as she tried to imagine what on Earth she was going to tell them.

Murdering Fiend

The dog came in from outside acting funny. Like, rejecting-a-bully-stick-and-favorite-liver-smelling treat type funny. I didn't think much of it. Just scratched the spot where her tail curlicues on her back, returned to my work.

But five minutes later she's at the door again, so I let her out. Time passes and she seems too quiet, so I go out, see her toying with something. Something bright red. Not a hapless cardinal who lingered too long pecking morsels from the tall grasses. Not that sort of red. The sort that has a bushy gray tail attached but little else. No feet, no head. I deduce this was once a squirrel. One of those kamikazes who relish high-stakes chases across the yard and up the oak tree to an astonishingly precise inch or two above her maximum, fully stretched on hind legs, height. Her being my dog. Kaida. Might as well go ahead and name the murdering fiend.

Jeeezizchrist, Kaida. What have you done? I shriek, as she chomps gluttonously on the remains like a starving cheetah on a gazelle. I stomp, hurl a ball, try to pull my alpha act. She's clearly unimpressed. So, I run inside, grab a paper bag and a wad of paper towels, dash back, wave the bag threateningly as I scoop up the limp carcass, which looks a bit like Dan'l Boone's hat before it was cleaned up nice and proper. She glances at me with a WTF, I'm trying to do my job here expression, grabs some morsel I've missed, crunches it noisily between powerful molars, and gulps it down with—is that a smile? Or just some perverse, crimson lip gloss?

Defeated, I carry off the forensic evidence, as if I'm merely toting a grocery bag containing a broken jar of crushed tomatoes. Walking to the nearby woods, where I plan to hurl the wretched thing over the hillside and off to eternity, my mind wanders to my first day of kindergarten.

My family lived across from the public elementary school, so I could see my house clearly. When the art teacher came in and told the class to paint a picture of their house, I was radiant with six-year-old confidence. After all, my house was right there. I painted with the kind of joy that comes from having liberal, bohemian parents who thought everything I did was great, and told me so, often. When I'd completed the task, I stood back waiting for Mrs. Grimm's praiseful assessment. And a smile did brighten her face as she held it up, looked across the street. *But this looks nothing like your house, little girl!* she declared cheerfully.

Meanwhile, back at my today home, the fiend is sniffing around, licking dolefully at the scene of the sacrifice. She gives up, walks belly-heavily to another part of the yard, not a moment wasted on the poison of disapproval, let alone a lifetime.

Golden Molar

Dr. Cruikshank patted her shoulder in the patronizing way people do with the elderly, as if she were a small child or puppy.

Hard to believe that filling held for sixty years, Mrs. Jones. Superb craftsmanship! We'll let the sedation work its magic. It'll feel like your evening martini, he added with a wink. *Make the root canal a positively pleasant experience.*

But Frances wasn't thinking about martinis or sedation. She was thinking about the sturdy crown her long-ago dentist installed that fateful year of her life, when she was just nineteen. Now that tooth was being reopened after six decades. It almost made her want to grab her purse—the one that devoured everything she placed in its dark interior—and bolt out of there, but for the searing pain in her mouth.

Her father had arranged everything back then. She would marry her thirty-year-old cousin, the one with no personality, whose parents were desperate to marry him off. There was the shotgun wedding, a deposit on a two-bedroom apartment she'd be sharing with the stranger who would become her husband, give her child a name, ask no questions, accept an accounting job at her father's company. Just three days before they'd wed, she went to the dentist with a terrible toothache. When she inhaled the nitrous and the dentist drilled into her tooth, she pictured the secret swirling into its depths, and when he sealed her golden molar, as he called it, she relaxed, convinced he'd buried it deep within the tooth, forever.

Dr. Cruikshank had a point. It was a bit like her nightly cocktail—a Manhattan, thank you very much, not a martini. Pleasant, delightful, then whoosh. Until he snapped the crown out and she felt a pop but no pain; heard herself deep within a tunnel slurrily pleading. *Stop, stop. Don't let it out.* As she drifted away again, she heard the dentist and his nurse, Nancy, laughing, laughing, then nothing.

Mrs. Jones? Can you hear us? Just take your time. You'll be a little woozy for a bit and here's a pill for later.

Frances lay on the cot, arm flung over her eyes, remembering the long dead husband she'd never loved, but who kept his promise to stand by her, raise her child with her. She thought, too, of the man she'd adored, her married lover with the Errol Flynn mustache, who flew for the Air Force, wore a fringed ivory-colored scarf, vanished when he learned she was pregnant. *What a cad he was—and what a fool was I.*

Yet, lying under the bright fluorescents in the chilly, betadine-scented room, she felt that terrible burden release—as if her ancient secret had been freed from its dark prison with that *pop!* never to return. She smiled to herself, enjoying the last flirty traces of anesthesia, remembering the tickle of that mustache on her neck, the teasing way he'd nibbled her skin before he disappeared forever.

The Mystery of His Words

"I love you, sweetheart. I'll never forget you." For years, I puzzled over my grandfather's last words to my grandmother. He wasn't a religious man, and it was he who was dying. Was he confused? Delirious? Eventually, I stopped wondering, stopped trying to apply logic. After all, contemplating the mystery and simplicity of his words has given me comfort ever since, as I'm sure it comforted my grandmother before she passed. Perhaps it was his way of saying that their love would endure, that their bond was so strong it didn't matter who was leaving, who was staying.

All's Well

Considering she was approaching 100, she was doing fine. She still planned dinner with her daughters most days, even put on a few pounds. She enjoyed having a cup of coffee with the neighbors at 4:00 every afternoon, nodding when they spoke of a son getting engaged or how expensive cherries were at the market. When her eldest son FaceTimed her, stroking his new silver-fox goatee proudly, and asked, "Do you know who I am?" she squinted at the screen. "Of course," she said without a trace of irony. "You're a very old man at the end of your life."

The Sweet Softness of Dates

She sits in her wicker chair, the one painted bright green because that's how she likes it. She lets the sweet softness of dates linger on her tongue, makes a small mound of pits on the seat next to her where the others won't see it and scold her for making a mess. The air coming in through the veranda windows smells of the sea and the bread bakery down below and exhaust from those damned motorbikes that roar the wrong way down the street day and night, day and night. Some poor dog is yowling—probably being chased by a snot-nosed kid with a stick whose family didn't raise him right.

Who am I? they ask. *Who are you? What year is it? Where were you born?* So many questions. Do they take me for a fool? I've survived war, a love that couldn't be and a marriage without it, children who left me to go here there and everywhere, a body once sturdy and beautiful that has grown stiff and feeble and fragile. So don't ask me who I am or what I remember. I am the air you breathe, the world you think of as yours. I am hands that have birthed a thousand babies, helped girls-barely-women in distress do what they felt they must, cooked countless meals when all I wanted was to put up my feet. These eyes have seen more than you'll ever know or understand. So don't ask me. Don't feed me. Don't try to make me sleep or walk in circles around the apartment in the building I built. Just leave me in the peace I've never known but have finally found. It is mine to take.

Acknowledgements

The author gratefully acknowledges the editors of the following publications in which these stories first appeared. In some cases, the versions in this collection may vary slightly from the published originals.

As In Life, *50-Word Stories*, The Breach, *Bending Genres*, Refuge, *Bright Flash Literary Review,* Snake. Taos New Mexico, *Citron Review,* Thousand-Watt Smile, *Cleaver Magazine,* Heart In A Box, *Dribble Drabble Review,* A Breath of Fresh Air and Too Late (originally titled Hylas and The Nymphs) *Ekphrastic Review,* Red Lava, *Ellipsis Zine,* I'm More My Father Than My Mother, *Emerge Literary Journal,* Blue, *Fictive Dream,* For Better, For Worse, Made For Walking, and In Alien Territory, *Flash Boulevard*, Three-Legged, *Litro Magazine,* She-Wolf, Aurora, and A Changed Man, *MacQueen's Quinterly,* Deep In The Woods, *Microfiction Monday,* Saturdays At the Souk, *New World Writing*, The Mystery of His Words, *New York Times-Tiny Love Stories,* It Might Have Happened Like This, *Pithead Chapel,* Murdering Fiend, *Potato Soup Journal,* The Sweet Softness of Dates and Between Springtime and Night, *Roi Fainéant,* Banging Pots and Pans, *Ruby Literary,* Silence Is a Stranger, *Six Sentences*, Golden Molar, *South Florida Poetry Journal,* All's Well, *The Drabble,* Chain of Fools, *Unbroken Journal*

I also acknowledge with deepest gratitude:

Meg Pokrass, in whose workshops some of my earliest flash and micro got its start, and who has supported my development as a writer of flash fiction in countless ways as well as fostering a dynamic, supportive, online flash and micro fiction community.

Kathy Fish, Sarah Freligh, Ann Hood, Hester Kaplan, Kathryn Kulpa, Lorette Luzajic, and Nancy Stohlman, in whose workshops many of these stories drew their first breaths of life. To all of you and to Rachel Laverdiere and Sherrie Flick for your editorial support and for doing so much for writers of flash both individually and in community. Your presence is a gift.

Pamela Painter, with whom I studied in the Creative Writing MFA program at Emerson College back in the day, and who more recently directed me toward the vibrant flash fiction community I'm immensely thankful to be a part of.

Thank you to all the devoted friends and family members who have read and critiqued my stories, reminded me to keep going even in times of doubt and inertia, and cheered me on when I was on a roll including:

Mikki Aronoff, dear friend and best writing/critiquing buddy imaginable.

Nasser Hajo—who has enthusiastically read everything I've ever written and made my stories look oh-so-fine on my website and who keeps life fun through it all.

Joanne Reynolds whose probing mind and constant support mean the world to me.

LiYana Silver—dearest sister and insightful reader who has been there all along the journey.

Bassil Silver-Hajo and Naseem Silver-Hajo, who make my life a joy, and whose creative paths often parallel my own in interesting, beautiful ways.

And to my wonderful online community of friends who have read and enjoyed my stories and offered many kind words and encouragement.

To Ariana Den Bleyker, editor and publisher extra-ordinaire, for exuberantly embracing the wild, wooly stories in "Wolfsong" and giving them a perfect home at ELJ Editions. And to the hard-working team at ELJ for all you do.

About the Author

Kathryn Silver-Hajo is an internationally published author, a Pushcart Prize, Best Small Fictions, and Best American Food Writing nominee whose fiction, creative nonfiction, and poetry appears in *Atticus Review, Bending Genres, Citron Review, Cleaver Magazine, Craft Literary, Emerge Literary Journal, Fictive Dream, Flash Boulevard, Litro Magazine, MacQueen's Quinterly, New World Writing, New York Times-Tiny Love Stories, Pithead Chapel, Ruby Literary, The Ekphrastic Review*, and other lovely places. Kathryn is a fiction reader for *Fractured Lit.* Her novel, *Roots of the Banyan Tree* is forthcoming in fall 2023 from *Juventud Press.* Kathryn lives in Providence, Rhode Island with her husband and sassy, curly-tailed pup, Kaya.

Discover more: kathrynsilverhajo.com. Follow her on Twitter: @KSilverHajo or Instagram: kathrynsilverhajo